W9-ACC-642

Dear Parent:

Congratulations! Your child is taking the first steps on an exciting journey. The destination? Independent reading!

STEP INTO READING® will help your child get there. The program offers five steps to reading success. Each step includes fun stories and colorful art. There are also Step into Reading Sticker Books, Step into Reading Math Readers, Step into Reading Write-In Readers, Step into Reading Phonics Readers, and Step into Reading Phonics First Steps! Boxed Sets—a complete literacy program with something for every child.

Learning to Read, Step by Step!

Ready to Read **Preschool–Kindergarten**
• big type and easy words • rhyme and rhythm • picture clues
For children who know the alphabet and are eager to begin reading.

Reading with Help **Preschool–Grade 1**
• basic vocabulary • short sentences • simple stories
For children who recognize familiar words and sound out new words with help.

Reading on Your Own **Grades 1–3**
• engaging characters • easy-to-follow plots • popular topics
For children who are ready to read on their own.

Reading Paragraphs **Grades 2–3**
• challenging vocabulary • short paragraphs • exciting stories
For newly independent readers who read simple sentences with confidence.

Ready for Chapters **Grades 2–4**
• chapters • longer paragraphs • full-color art
For children who want to take the plunge into chapter books but still like colorful pictures.

STEP INTO READING® is designed to give every child a successful reading experience. The grade levels are only guides. Children can progress through the steps at their own speed, developing confidence in their reading, no matter what their grade.

Remember, a lifetime love of reading starts with a single step!

For Dad—D.U.
For Krista: the mom who really is a pirate—S.G.

www.stepintoreading.com

Educators and librarians, for a variety of teaching tools, visit us at
www.randomhouse.com/teachers

Library of Congress Cataloging-in-Publication Data
Underwood, Deborah.
Pirate Mom / by Deborah Underwood ; illustrated by Stephen Gilpin. — 1st ed.
p. cm. — (Step into reading. Step 3 book)
SUMMARY: When a hypnotist convinces Pete's mother that she is a pirate, Pete tries to find a way to turn her back into a regular parent.
ISBN 0-375-83323-4 (pbk.) — ISBN 0-375-93323-9 (lib. bdg.)
[1. Pirates—Fiction. 2. Hypnotism—Fiction. 3. Mothers and sons—Fiction.
4. Humorous stories—Fiction.]
I. Gilpin, Stephen, ill. II. Title. III. Series.
PZ7.U4193Pir 2006
[E]—dc22 2005023910

Printed in the United States of America

10 9 8 7 6 5 4 3 2

First Edition

STEP INTO READING®

Pirate Mom

by Deborah Underwood
illustrated by Stephen Gilpin

Random House New York

The Hypno-Trance

"Arrr!" said Pete.

He swished his pirate sword.

He jumped on his pirate bed.

"Come downstairs, Pirate Pete,"

called his mom.

Pete told Teddy to guard the loot.

Pete ran downstairs.

"Will you play pirates with me?"

he asked.

Pete's mom said no.

Pete's mom never wanted

to play pirates.

She did not like pirates.

She said pirates were not polite.

But she had a nice surprise.

"Wow!" Pete said.
"Tickets to see
the Amazing Marco today!"

Pete and his mom
went to the show.
The lights dimmed.
The crowd got quiet.
"Ladies and gentlemen—
the Amazing Marco!"
boomed a voice
from behind them.

The Amazing Marco pulled
a rabbit out of his hat.
"Ooooh!" said the crowd.

The Amazing Marco cut
Zelda, his helper, in half.
"Aaaah!" said the crowd.

It was time for Marco's
most amazing trick . . .
the Hypno-Trance!

The Amazing Marco picked
Pete's mom.
He told her she was getting sleepy.
Pete's mom closed her eyes.
"What should she be
when she wakes up?"
Marco asked the crowd.

"A pirate!" Pete called.

The Amazing Marco turned
to Pete's mom.

"When I clap my hands,
you will be a pirate," he said.
He clapped his hands.

Pete's mom opened her eyes.
"Arrr!" she said.
"I am a salty old pirate.
Give me your loot!"
Everyone cheered.

Suddenly Zelda ran onstage.
"Your wife is having the baby!"
Zelda told the Amazing Marco.
"Yikes!" cried Marco.
"The show is over, folks!"
He ran off the stage.

"Wait!" Pete called.

"My mom is still a pirate!"

"Oh, that wears off
most of the time,"
said Zelda.

"*Most* of the time?"
cried Pete.

But Zelda was gone.

Pirate Problems

Pete and Pirate Mom walked home.

It was not easy.

Pirate Mom tried to fight

with Ms. Reed.

She called Mr. Collins a bilge rat.

She stole underwear
from Mrs. Burt's clothesline.

Pete was glad
to get Pirate Mom inside.
Pirate Mom fell asleep
on the couch.

Pete hoped the pirate spell
would wear off.
He went out to play.

An hour later, he came home.

"Yikes!" he cried.

A pirate flag flew over his house.

Pirate Mom stood in the yard.

She wore an eye patch

and a pirate head scarf.

Pete's parrot sat on her shoulder.

Pirate Mom swished
a wooden spoon at the mailman.
"Arrr!" said Pirate Mom.
"Arrr!" said the parrot.
"Arrrrrrgh!" said Pete.

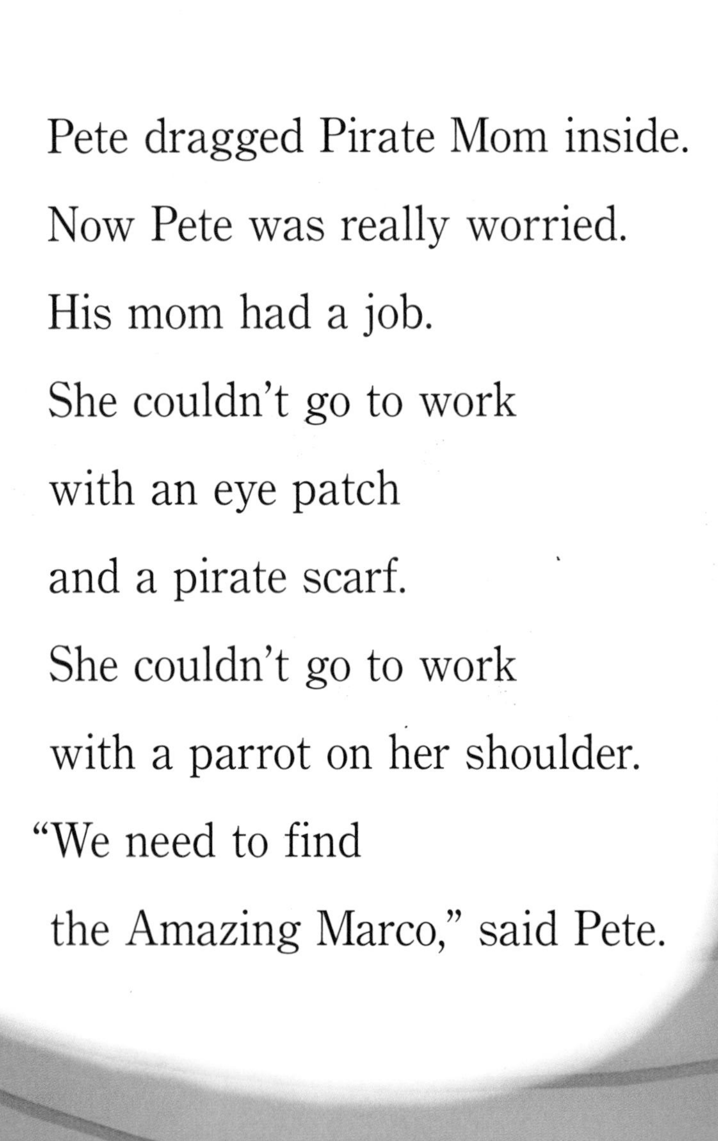

Pete dragged Pirate Mom inside.
Now Pete was really worried.
His mom had a job.
She couldn't go to work
with an eye patch
and a pirate scarf.
She couldn't go to work
with a parrot on her shoulder.
"We need to find
the Amazing Marco," said Pete.

Ding-dong!

The doorbell rang.

Pete told Pirate Mom

to wait in the kitchen.

"You scurvy lad!

I will not!" said Pirate Mom.

Ding-dong! Ding-dong!

Pete thought fast.

"There is loot in the kitchen."

"Shiver me timbers!

Why didn't you say so?"

Pirate Mom ran out of the room.

Pete peeked out the door.
A bunch of people
pushed past him.
They had come
for a PTA meeting.
There was a crash
in the kitchen.
"What was that?"
asked a man.

Pirate Mom burst through the door.

She waved a frying pan in the air.

"Yo ho ho!" she said.

"Give me your loot!"

"Oh my," said the people.

Pete thought fast again.
"Mom thinks you should have
a costume party," Pete said.
"It's a good way to raise money
for the school."

“What a wonderful idea!”
said one of the men.
“All in favor say ‘Aye.’”
“Aye!” said the people.

"Aye!" said the parrot.

"Arrr!" said Pirate Mom.

Marco's Surprise

Pete had to find the Amazing Marco.
Marco's wife had just had a baby.
So Pete took Pirate Mom
to the hospital.

He asked a nurse
where the Amazing Marco was.
“No pirates!” said the nurse.
“Wait here,” Pete told Pirate Mom.

The Amazing Marco
was with his new son,
the Fabulous Harold.
"Come quick!" Pete said.
"My mom is still a pirate!"

They went to find Pirate Mom.
The nurse was hiding
under his desk.
Pirate Mom was gone!

Pete and Marco heard
a voice down the hall.
"Hand over the loot!"

Pirate Mom was talking
to two men.
"Draw your swords,
you yellow-bellied bandits!"
said Pirate Mom.
"We are not bandits.
We are doctors," they said.

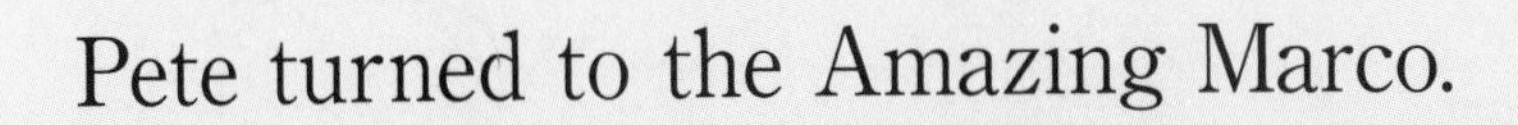

Pete turned to the Amazing Marco.

"I like pirates," Pete said.

"But it is hard having
a pirate for a mom."

"Oh dear," said Marco.

"I am very sorry."

Marco snuck up on Pirate Mom.
He told her she was getting sleepy.
He told her it was time
to be Pete's mom again.
He clapped his hands.

She woke up.
"Where are we?
What happened?"
asked Pete's mom.

“Marco turned you
into a pirate,” said Pete.
“Don’t be silly,” said Pete’s mom.
She bumped into a wheelchair.
“Maybe you should take off
your eye patch,” Pete said.

Pete's mom put her hand
on her face.
She felt the eye patch.
"Oh my," she whispered.

The next day, Pete found

a letter under the door.

It was from the Amazing Marco.

His mom read the letter.

Sorry for all the trouble.

Please accept this gift.

Two bits of paper fell out.

They were tickets for
the Amazing Marco's next show.
"Oh no!" said Pete's mom.
"Oh no!" said Pete.
"Arrr!" said the parrot.

water damage on last few pages.
AM WGRL-HQ 12.16